SHE GAVE ME HER
NUMBER
TO ANOTHER
DIMENSION

John M3 Frame

2020

I want you to know that now that I know everything I know, the words flow like magic, like the day it all started.

I was pretending chatting, but what I was really doing was looking at the girls who were entering university, it was like a hobby, sometimes I followed them and tried to talk to them, other times I only saw them pass by, but I didn't expect that big surprise, the girl who came in with her model pose, the girl with brown hair, white skin, sensual eyes and a flirtatious face, was the woman of my life, although I had been very close to speaking to her, literally a few inches from her lips, I hadn't been able to do it, well I didn't do it that day, but I received news that made my heart happy forever.

She was waiting for someone and she seemed a little nervous, she held her purse in her left hand, then in her right hand, then her left, and so on about ten times, at first I assumed the purse was heavy, but when she pulled out her phone and held the purse up with just one finger, I changed my mind

I kept looking at her because something told me that that day had a surprise in store for me; maybe, she would declare her love to me and make my life take a different turn.

At first, I received a bucket of cold water, my illusions fell several meters underground, I lost sight of her for a moment, and she was making out with a guy.

I turned around and was willing to forget about the world, but one word, just one word saved me.

"what's wrong with you?" she said.

I immediately looked at her and she pushed the guy away and ran off.

I was so happy, my soul returned to my body, now if I could breathe easy, not because she left or because she had pushed the guy, but because now I knew that she was available.

Best of all, she was highly selective, and I really like that about a woman, because feeling unique, special to a person is everything.

It is something very gratifying, of course that at that time I didn't understand it in the same way as I see it now, but if it was clear that she was available and that I had the opportunity to hold her in my arms, that was the best news I received while I was training in espionage.

I secretly went through all the corridors of the university, she came out of the bathroom, she looked as if she kept a secret, and she kept something in her purse, now I understand it, but until then, it seemed something strange, I was watching her without her seeing me; she looked at once towards the toilet door, her lips moved as if she were very nervous, she met with a girl, she quickly took her by the arm, turned her and they went almost running in the direction of the stairs towards the first floor, I stared into the toilet, because the door suddenly closed.

I approached carefully, because I couldn't rush into the female toilet, I was ready to go in, I already had my hand on the door handle, and I almost screamed when someone interrupted me by touching my shoulder.

"this is Ladies toilet, this is ladies toilet!," one of the professors told me.

I think that was a warning, that it was time to go to class.

The professor looked at me with great annoyance, and as if saying go to hell.

I just smiled.

"You are beautifully, provocative like my favorite food," I said.

I don't know why I dared to say it, I felt that something had changed in me with just the news that the love of my life was available.

The professor wrinkled her eyes, adjusted her miniskirt.

I was looking at her closely, and she smiled when entered the female toilet.

My reaction wasn't much different when I entered class, as I would expect everyone was so stiff sitting similarly, in the same hard and flat chairs.

"The sky turned blue, and the sun winked at it," I said aloud, looking at the physics professor.

In her first reaction, she would have wanted to throw the marker at me, because she took it at an angle of ninety degrees and moved her hand in a pendulum motion, but something made her change her mind when everyone burst into laughter, one of the classmates had to go to the toilet, because she had a fit of laughter.

"Let's see, funny man, go to the board and draw the parabolic movement," the professor said while trying not to laugh.

I was just a short walk away from sitting down in my place, which is a chair after the row facing the board, one of the classmates looked at me flirtatiously, she even gently brought her pen to her mouth and winked at me.

"Mr. humorist," the professor told me, stretching out her hand as if she wanted to propose to me.

Now everyone was looking at me as if I were the life of the party, for a long time, I had always been silent and everyone nicknamed me like the most serious guy from the university, knowing that she was available for me, was a source of power, in that instant I remembered her beautiful words.

"what's wrong with you?" and so I told the professor.

That was where she couldn't stand it, she laughed so loud and strong that the fit of laughter took everyone to the toilet, some in the hallways, others lay down occupying several chairs.

I kept the marker in my hands, which promptly cleared my mind, I woke up from the dream I was in, I remembered the concepts of physics from last semester, when I saw this subject for the first time, I drew the parabolic movement along with all the formulas , and with a happy smile, remembering the famous phrase of the love of my life.

The professor was the last to recover from laughing, when she entered the classroom, I was already in my place.

She entered with the seriousness that characterizes her, it seemed that she didn't want to see us in the face, she entered looking towards the board, she saw the drawing of the parabolic movement.

Perhaps it was because the draw was longer than it was wide, or because of the happy faces, that she quickly put both hands to her mouth, remained static for a moment, then took a step to one side as if heading to the exit.

And when we saw her, she was laughing, she was trying not to make any noise, but again her laugh was quite loud and special.

The classmate who was next to me was the second to laugh, as she moved move side to side.

That was the beginning of the end, the beginning of a mass hysteria and the end of the class.

I slept like a baby with so much laughter, I woke up with a lot of energy, I even wanted to take a shower, of course I shower every day, but it made me want to shower with cold water, that was a kind of ritual or preparation for what it would be like that day.

My smile didn't disappear even when I brushed my teeth, which were whiter than normal because I could see them in their entirety, that was a good sign, also if she was available, she was for me, my heart told me, beating stronger when I was thinking of her.

"Hello, life is beautiful" I said to a beautiful girl who was coming out of college.

She ran her hand through her hair slowly, it was something unique, she smiled at me too.

I had a hunch that I was going to meet her again and it was exactly like that, something out of the ordinary, turning into something fantastic and not very credible for those who are skeptical.

The first place I entered was the cafeteria, because I

really wanted to eat something sweet, when the door opened, my eyes couldn't believe it, there she was as if she were waiting for me, she stayed watching me until a group of girls passed by, they were laughing at a bad joke, that's what they said when they passed my path.

I looked back at her, although she wasn't longer looking at me, she was putting on makeup, that was an invitation, the confirmation that she was also dying for me, in the end I decided not to buy the chocolate, I had enough sweet with seeing her, her lips every time she delineated with lipstick were a call for my desire to kiss her, when she crossed her legs, I knew it, it was now or never, I had to take advantage of my good streak, my smile that had brought me to a very good grade in physics.

I clarified my voice like singers do, a guy, or a professor, now I'm not sure his reason for being at the university, he was watching me while I tuned my voice, I thought it bothered him, but in a few seconds, he copied the same techniques, surely, he also had to prepare for something similar.

When I finished tuning my voice, I observed her carefully, she was now laughing in a very flirtatious way, that was the green light, the signal to act or shut up forever.

When I approached, she stared at me, smiled lovingly at me, then slowly stood up, took a paper, folded it very delicately, then kissed it, turned to me and gave it to me.

she only took a few seconds for give me what would be

the greatest treasure of my entire existence.

she almost kissed me on the first contact, it would have been very romantic and not believable for the most skeptical and serious audiences, not to say unpleasant audience.

I stared at the silhouette of her lips on the sheet of paper, I also stared at her when she flirtatiously walks for me, as she left the cafeteria.

I kissed her, kissing the silhouette of her lips on the paper, I kept it very close to my heart and my smile was even more noticeable.

For four nights and almost five days the smile lasted on my face, they were the best moments of my existence, the second night I dreamed that she was sitting on the stern of a yacht, she had a yellow bathing suit, at first I saw her swimsuit like phosphorescent, but it was because the sunlight wasn't perfectly graduated, I woke up, drank some water, did a warm-up, threw myself into bed as if it were a pool, I kept sleeping face down, there I began to see her swimsuit on the color that it was, very pleasing to the eye, it highlighted her breasts, her waist, what struck me the most was her smile, her teeth shone with freshness, I went over to give her a kiss, but I woke up and it was already eight o'clock in the morning.

Until that moment that number didn't represent anything to me, simply that it was late enough not to bathe, but just my face.

The third night, she was on the beach, she was watching me, I don't remember what I was supposedly doing, but she was smiling at me in a very sensual way, her hair was blowing over her face, she looked too beautiful, I approached slowly towards her, and someone passed between us with a large sign that only had a number drawn, stared at me and then ran away.

I stared at the number, when I turned to her, I woke up again, this time it was nine o'clock, I didn't pay attention to that either, because I had class at ten, I managed to bathe and even shave.

The last night, she was dressed differently but just as sexy, a tight-fitting blouse, a shorts fitting to her silhouette, she was leaning against the wall of a balcony, she was watching me as if she were insinuating herself, I decided to approach her without mishap, she stared into my eyes, I did too, we stayed like this for several seconds, then she looked forward, I did the same, she sighed, and said seven; that caused me a lot of grace, I laughed like I never did, not even in the class that had to be postponed due to the collective fits of laughter, I took a deep breath and was ready to kiss her, the alarm clock rang, I opened my eyes, and I saw the number seven .

There it seemed a bit strange, but I kept sleeping in case I managed to kiss her, because that day I didn't have class in the morning.

That dream was something strange like the number, I didn't see her face well, she no longer had a white blouse, nor shorts, nor underwear, I got hot, my voice trembled, however I took the first step, but I slipped and I woke up, I was sweating and with my underpants down, I didn't see the clock, I stayed for more than an hour looking at the ceiling, trying to remember that beautiful dream.

After all this trajectory, from that story between the two,

it could be said that we already had a fairly long relationship of days and nights of being intertwined, of being in sync.

There was something that made me lose my smile completely, but it wasn't the romantic film, instead it produced another extremely important effect, the film began like all love stories, with caresses, with kisses, with some risque scenes, comedy scenes, crazy comedy, sex scenes, but I didn't expect that ending, in the middle, the girl looked lacking in seriousness like those little girls who bite a chocolate and then throw it away, because she didn't like the way it become after a tremendous bite, instead the protagonist began to act like me, I saw myself on the screen, a little taller than the protagonist, because he was short, a little more handsome than the protagonist too, although he picks up women, I pick up women in the more easy way, but I felt identified at that moment with him when he saw her eyes, he squeezed her hand and he confessed that he loved her.

So far it was the best movie of my life, but the mess began, she got complicated, the story followed the thread making her disappear without leaving any trace, there I also coincided with the protagonist when he wondered what the hell happened with that beautiful girl, she was in my arms and left as if by magic.

At that point I almost turned off the television, but I also wanted to know what happened to the girl, of course she was a model and also an actress on a YouTube channel. It is clear that she went to record an episode on a remote island, because the recording studio in her house was canceled because the graphic designer went on vacation, super clear, however, I wanted to confirm it, see it, feel it.

The final part began and nothing was known about the woman's whereabouts, the protagonist made a relentless search making thousands of calls, in addition to visiting the apartment, he also communicated with the owners of YouTube, but nothing at all.

I was already desperate, more than half an hour had passed and this man didn't advance in his investigation, until he remembered that she had given him a letter before leaving, he held it in his hands for several minutes, and I knew it from his face, he would never read it after he called the girl's parents, he told them everything they had done, among other more intimate things, and so it was.

The protagonist runs onto a terrace, approached the edge of a fourth floor, put his hand in his pocket, moved his fingers as if taking something out and of course the letter fell accidentally.

Of course, that was a masterful move, if it weren't for the fact that the film ends tragically, she had left the instructions for him to so that they would meet in a wonderful place, days later the protagonist was consumed in a depression and he tried to recover the letter, but never couldn't do this.

That is why I took action on the matter, I wasn't going to allow something similar to happen to me, I looked for the pants that were still in the dirty clothes, the despair at not finding the piece of paper made my smile disappear completely, and after more than two hours looking for it, I found it on the nightstand just as I went to set the alarm for the nap take every afternoon, which is how I get rid of the world.

I postponed the sacred nap; he had the living images of the protagonist crying and thrown to grief.

But first I had to prepare, that first call is like the first impression, I saw a movie in which women decided who to go out with, according to the tone of the man's voice when he called them to confirm the first date, that is another tragic movie, anyway, I needed to coordinate every detail, I wrote the lines that I was going to say, I almost can't decide if I said "hi" or "hello, how are you?" or if I went straight without any monotonous introduction, in the end I decided for a hi, to be nice above all , is one of my mottos, I brushed my teeth three times, maybe what I heard on the street is true, a guy said to another, she detect my breath on the phone, and immediately she hung up, I saw his face suffering and alcoholic, yet I brushed a fourth time just in case.

It was time to try the exercises of a vocal technique course, I only attended one class, however, this class was the most important, those exercises are perfect, I was warming up my voice, I also did some yoga exercises, fifty squats, that last exercise wasn't I know if it serves that purpose however it's the first thing that came to mind

After several hours I had everything ready, my finger millimeters away from pressing the call button.

I wasn't able, I did another round of squats, again I warmed up my voice and I remembered the face of the protagonist, there it was already clear.

And I called her.

I was waiting to hear her voice

"this number is not available" I listened to the voice of a recording.

I checked the numbers over and over again, nothing strange was seen at first glance, I called ten more times, always the same message, so I decided to observe carefully, that was the beginning of this great path to the truth, not exactly as I imagined, but it was much better, I realized that she had deliberately written some numbers in a different way, a two seemed like a one, a nine a four and so I made some possible combinations, I'm believing that she was doing it to make me understand that she is a difficult girl and a true golden award.

That day I called forty numbers, of which I discarded thirty eight, I already had two possible numbers, one was an answering machine in which the voice was very similar to her, that message misled me, I ran in search of the paper where I had written down my lines and it had fallen on the floor, after that incident I wrote the lines on the palm of my hand, as everyone does.

The other was a little girl who answered the phone, at first, I came to think that she had finished bathing, and that is why she had such a thin tone of voice, but when she told me

"She kept the phone in my room, because I realized she was taking one of my mirrors"

I was silent.

"Please call her at night, ok" she added and hung up

I changed my daily routine, the nap was replaced by hours
of calls, if this count as experience I already had enough
of a customer service operator, my patience was seen to
the limits of overflowing, in a cauldron of anger when they
hung up on me when I had the half the words in the mouth,
a man faked a girl's voice.

"Hi, I'm the one you are looking for," he said.

My inner self was about to tell him, his jar voice doesn't
resemble that of a woman, much less that of a little girl, but
I held myself, held my breath for fifteen seconds.

"big m***********, go to the s***" he said and hung up

I never knew what happened in those fifteen seconds, I
left the phone next to the television, I closed my eyes, took
a deep breath, I counted very slowly, I think that in total it
was like fifty or sixty real seconds, the fact is that people are
very strange, like the movie that was playing on tv, it was
about two guys who liked to talk to each other swearing,
but it didn't end well, another tragic story, because in the
end those jokes turned into something serious, they hurt

each other sentimentally and never they turned to talk.

That was one of the peculiarities of the calls, mostly women answered with a harmonious voice, they all looked alike, I came to think that maybe I was dialing the same number over and over again, but no, all the numbers were different; Those girls had the same accent, I imagined them with the same clothes, eating the same, doing the same exercises for a flat abdomen, a good butt and a good body.

All of them without exception stayed talking for exactly three minutes, all of them hung up after three minutes.

"Hello," I would tell them.

"Hellooo, how are you?" they were saying.

There was a brief pause, then they continued.

"who am I talking to?" they said followed by a giggle in ellipsis.

Since I needed to verify that it was her, I prepared a message for everyone, as a key that only she and I would know.

"I read the message, I'm enumerating and coding" I said to them.

Without exception they all laughed as if someone was tickling them.

"Oh no, who am I talking to?" they said again.

I was very prepared with another message.

"I discovered the four and the nine, the two is missing" I added.

At that moment they had a fit of laughter, it was heard how her phone jumped with them.

"Oh no, seriously who am I talking to?" they said again.

At that point it was already the last message he had prepared to confirm that she was her.

"I'm figure out everything, your numbers are the riddles of my heart," I told them with a serious and slow tone so that they understood the message.

"Oh no, tell me the truth, who am I talking to?" they said with an insinuating tone.

Then there was a silence of exactly ten seconds.

"Call me later, take care of yourself, kisses," they said as if they were hiding from someone.

I continued in silence, I listened to their breaths for ten more seconds and at exactly three minutes, absolutely all of them, they hung up.

I was like that for several days, between combinations of calls of thirty seconds or less to some in which the conversation flowed even in a good friendship, I met Brenda who later would also help me to decipher other things.

Of course, it was something pleasant at first, but the hours began to pass, the numbers seemed eternal, they were confused with the numbers on my watch, now I was going to bed at four in the morning and at six I had to be awake again.

At that rate it was going to end as a story I saw on YouTube, it was about telepathy, a small but old boy, that is to say, short in stature, he was sure he had telepathic abilities capable of influencing people's behavior, and one day , he tried it by seducing a super model without even having spoken to her before, not even being close to her, only seeing her from his computer screen, the super model on her wedding day confirmed that in a second she felt desires for him, which was a true love, so far fine, the story deserved for an Oscars awards, it had the best talent, it was innovative and of course the girl was a super model, but a trainee entered the story, it was a guy who had just graduated from high school, He received exact instructions from that little man of unique and unrepeatable wisdom.

The happy guy, hard training for days, but didn't obtain the expected results, he decided to double his efforts, and also sacrifice his nights, in a short time he could hardly move from sleep, but that wasn't the problem, it was that he hadn't achieved any result.

The little man found out, and since his reputation was at stake, he visited him, asked him which girl he wanted to attract, he showed him a video, she was a YouTube superstar, at first glance she seemed super available, given to meet new people, simple and fun.

The guy looked at him as if deciphering what he wanted to say to him.

The little man shook his head.

"did you read the fine print?" he said to him

The guy rubbed his chin like he was remembering something then his face flushed and he looked at the floor.

So far so good, the story would have a happy ending, I said to myself, because right now he will tell him the secret or something that he forgot to apply and they will marry, but the man said:

"There are only beings on the planet capable of resisting the power of telepathy, these beings belong to another dimension, they are beings capable of transforming, mutating in a matter of seconds, they are the You%%%%%%, the influ$$$$$ and the ... "

the guy's mouth opened wide.

"And now what do I do?" he said.

The little man very wise in every way, he said

"If you can't fight them ..."

"Umm" the guy said.

After ten years, the guy mastered the art of these beings, and at that moment he realized that he is in love with a super model, she had been his best friend ten years ago.

And now I felt like the guy, I had sleepless nights, I had done all the possible combinations and I had nothing, I fell asleep between so many numbers, the paper sheets were scattered throughout the room, when I woke up, my saliva had left a bridge between several paper sheets overlapping the numbers, making a few digits clear, then I wrote them on a clean sheet and observed the number she had given me, they were the same digits, but in a different order, was it a coincidence? Or a signal ?, I chose the second.

After such a revealing clue the universe put in front of me, I got a brilliant idea, one that would begin to unravel the puzzle of numbers.

The day she gave me her most precious treasure, the secret that she guarded with suspicion, she held a book in her hands before looking me in the eye and hinting that I was the guardian of her mysteries.

I was practicing telepathy for a minute, but it seems that it doesn't work, it's time to forget that silly story, it was already enough of lost and wasted loves of life.

What was clear to me is that I had to act now, or I would lose it forever, according to what I could guess, the numbers are showing a big timer, and I had approximately three days left.

Three days to solve this riddle, without further ado I went to the library, as I was a friend of the librarian, she let me see the books she had requested or read.

I had to make sure which book she was reading, or if

there was more than one book that would allow me to find clues about the digits, that I had written on the palms of my hands.

"I don't know whether to give you the information, why do you need it?" my friend told me.

I had known her for a long time, I looked into her eyes, and I knew exactly what she wanted.

"But... I get a reward or something?" she told me

I showed her my palm as a sign that I'm going to buy you something and I'll be back, but she kept looking at the numbers, I don't know what happened, but she told me:

"Wait don't buy anything,"

I had my feet pointed towards the exit, it was uncomfortable to return to the position from before and pretend that none of the previous minutes had passed.

She stared at the numbers longer than my hand could resist in the same position, I was holding my breath, I felt my legs shake, I felt my face burning, my forehead full of sweat.

"Done," she said

It was one of the best sensations in my whole life, I felt light, without unencumbers, now I felt energetic and ready for everything.

"what do you want?" I told.

My friend smiled, her dimples on her cheeks make her look too cute, nice, and a good person.

"I'll be right back," she said

I stared at her carefully, it would be the dimples in her cheeks, her laugh, or maybe what she figured out of the numbers, but now she looked prettier, she walked more straight , elegant, well, I sat on one of the chairs available, there were actually a lot of available ones, there was only one other person besides me and my friend.

A guy dressed in black, with medium-long hair was bent over, I think he was writing, no, he was drawing.

"Here it is," my friend told me

I jumped in shock, but she looked at me and the dimples in her smile reassured me again.

She gave me the records of the books that she had requested, only one book appeared in the registry and it was the same day that she gave me the number, such a coincidence cannot be true, my friend gave me the book without paperwork, the book was of conspiracies, a mystery novel, in which a spy had infiltrated information in some mathematical games, after seeing the cover of the book lying on my bed, again I fell asleep again, but this time the saliva wasn't the key.

I started to read the book, the first few pages caught me, I could see her smile as I read each word out loud, but there were so many numbers on the floor that I couldn't concentrate, so I left it on the table where I put the important objects.

When I picked up some sheets, my hands were filled with black ink, I didn't realize it until it occurred to me to look at the numbers, I wanted to check again if there was something hidden, that the first two hundred times, I couldn't see, at that moment the phone vibrated, and I almost dropped the sheet of paper.

That was a blessing, because when I saw the number again, it stained with the ink that I had on my fingers, I brought the page a little closer to see it well, the marks looked like parentheses and commas.

And whoa!

He had begun to decipher the puzzle, the numbers weren't from a phone number, nor were the combinations from a safe, nor were they born dates, they were coordinates, no number was there at random, they all had a reason to be there.

I already knew that they were coordinates, the first thing that occurred to me was that they were from somewhere, I tried to translate them into the language of latitude and longitude, I was doing the combinations, but all the places were unreal, one pointed to a place in Patagonia, another at the north pole, the last one I checked in the middle of the ocean.

For some reason I remembered the calculus teacher, just bringing her to my mind gave me such a panic that I turned off my brain for half an hour, put on the headphones and the song "Mission: Impossible theme song" played instantly, during the half hour I was sailing in a dream.

She was wearing a very low-cut black dress, it was like an elegant party because I looked at my clothes and I was wearing a suit with a tie, I looked around and all the men were dressed the same as me; She drank from her glass and set it on one of the trays that the servers hold fairly balanced, then came over to me, stroking my chin with one of her fingers.

"You're my best book," she said me

Her voice made me shiver with heat.

She smiled, and walked off in a very provocative way.

When the song was over, I tried to remember the shape of the dress, but something darkened is part of my memory, I rubbed my chin.

"I'm her best book," I said quietly.

Of course! the book, I ran and almost grabbed it like that with the ink in my hands, it would have been some incident that might have cost me a friendship and a few bills, I wiped my hands with another sheet that I found on the floor.

And whoa!

Now I hadn't only one clue but two, it was a conscience or a master move of destiny; one of them pointed to a specific page of the book, where the mathematical table that the spy had designed to infiltrate the message was printed, more coincidences, or everything was linked.

I called Brenda who had just told me that she was an excellent math and a bit more at solving puzzles, which she loved it. She said it in a somewhat sensual tone.

I didn't pay much attention to that, from experience I knew that many women have that tone of voice by default, it's as if they had listened to the same recording as children and learned it without realizing it, an effect similar to the television, the music or videos on YouTube, in any case I didn't give it importance, I transferred the numbers to a clean sheet and left them in the book in case between both of us, we could read it quickly.

On the street I was repeating the numbers, in case I could decipher something else, but I ended up learning them by heart and as if they were a pre-kindergarten song, something strange was happening, I took a deep breath and knocked on the door of Brenda's apartment, and opened at the slightest touch.

"Come in and relax" she said in a very suggestive tone.

So far completely normal, that confirmed to me that she

had indeed listened to the recording, and I just opened the door.

At that point I thought I had the wrong apartment.

It was half dark, there was a lit candle on a small table next to the living room, next to two glasses with some kind of pink drink, and several slices of pizza.

My mind tried to explain coherently, but was left in exclamation when I saw some paper hearts that decorated the room, they were adorned with lights in the shape of stars.

"Brenda?"

I said in a doubtful voice, I think she knew.

"Oh yeah, silly, make yourself comfortable, this may take a while" she said from some unknown point in the apartment.

Having confirmed, I came in to the living room walking slowly, when I got close to the candles, my attention went to the hearts, these had numbers in the middle, I looked at the walls and I saw more numbers, I approached the candle to see the numbers that I had written down, because at that point and after repeating them so much I had completely forgotten them.

While looking for the numbers, I noticed a very pleasant perfume smell very close to me.

"Hi," Brenda said as she hugged me around the waist.

I just got really ticklish, I remembered the physics class, and I almost laughed, I managed to control myself I took a step forward and turned around, because I wanted to see her.

She was looking at me smiling, and there I saw it clear, she hadn't heard the recording, she came with the recording in her genes, her light blue eyes, her smooth skin without any imperfection, her eyelashes bent with the charisma of her laugh, her very fine white teeth, apart from her pink sweater, everything about her matched that tone of voice.

"Relax and enjoy," she said me

I didn't know whether to show her the numbers at once, but when she hugged me again, I didn't know what to say, we sat in front of that exquisite pizza that also had a heart shape, and I could finally remember the numbers, and they were the same ones that appeared on the walls, in the hearts, and on the table as decorations.

This was either another coincidence or another sign of the truth.

I decided I had to act.

"These are the numbers," I said showing her the book

She took the book in her hands, danced, spined several times.

"I love this book," she said

"Yes, please can you help me decipher page 911 specifically at the figure number 11," I said modulating very quickly.

She stared at me without saying anything, then moved quite suggestively.

"OK, just give me a second," she said as she left the living room.

I kept seeing the numbers, the candles that dazzled my eyes, I blinked several times trying not to see the bright point, but then I realized that the bright point was like a separation of thousands.

And wow!

I had another part of the puzzle solved, since I didn't have a pen, I stood up.

"Brenda?" I said to know where I was, with the revealing light in my eyes, I saw everything else dark.

"If you want, come," she said me

That was good news, from the tone she used, I knew it was because she had discovered something great, but before that piece of pizza was looking at me closely.

"Are you coming?" she said me

"I'm coming," I said savoring that delicious homemade pizza.

"What?" she said

I told her the same again and again, as many times as were required to finish my slice of pizza and hers, I don't know, but something told me that she had no appetite.

"Hu Hu, are you coming?" she said me.

I drank the drink, it was like many drinks mixing, I could only distinguish whiskey, white wine, champagne, and some kind of cocktail, I approached her, but everything was so dark.

"Marco," I said

"Polo," she said in an extremely sexy voice.

My feet immediately followed the voice, she was standing trying to remove her blouse.

"Would you help me?" she said me

"Sure," I said to her

She was in her underwear, carefully helping her remove her blouse, which was stuck with her arm and head.

"Thank you," she said, looking into my eyes.

"I wanted to know if you have already read page 911 in figure 11," I said very quickly.

She looked me in the eye, then took out a calculator from the nightstand, looked at page 911 and table 11, did some calculations on a scientific calculator, then brought in several books, copied various formulas, drew various graphs, then wrote something at the end of the page where the numbers were, I stared into her eyes.

I wanted to thank her for everything she was doing for me, I hugged her, she caressed me gently, I don't know why, if it was the perfume, her aroma, her caresses, seeing her in her underwear, feeling the softness of her bed, or the candles that still I saw, but she attracted me a lot.

"Relax and enjoy," she said me as she brought my hands to her hips.

Her tone of voice at that point was the highest in sensuality, she had undoubtedly been born with that talent, and it was obvious that she had practiced it a lot.

"We have all the numbers for us," she said me in that same tone.

There I kissed her, she happily reciprocated, we made love all night, even on top of all the stained numbers, at the foot of the candles, on each of the sofas, leaning against the walls where the numbers were and on some blank sheets of paper.

I woke up with hearts flying above my head, like it was a dream, except that one of the star-shaped lights was over my mouth and the movement of the hearts was a simple optical confusion.

She was completely asleep, sometimes she stretched out her arms on the mattress.

"Come in, relax and enjoy," she said in a too sexy voice.

I looked at her carefully, she looked so happy even as if she was smiling, whatever that dream was, she was enjoying it a lot, I let her enjoy, I slowly slipped under this blanket that pretended to be heaven.

Now I had understood the shape of the lights that surrounded her, in truth she took great care in the details, she's a master in deciphering the mathematical riddles of life, and she was also born with the gift of that particular tone that captivates and hypnotizes, and she's a good friend.

But something surprised me more, when I went to look for the book, the sheets fell, I thought I had seen everything she wrote, but there was a message between the lines, this message had been in front of my nose since she made the calculations, I was a few hours late, and every time I have less time to find the answer to the numbers.

I repeated the message over and over again, so that it would stick in my mind.

"law that governs the universe in all dimensions" the message said

I repeated it so many times that my mouth was dry, then I looked at the table that had the candles, I saw that there was still a little drink in one of the glasses, I approached trying not to make noise, I did not want her to wake up from her dream so pleasant, her soft moans were adorned with a lot of sensuality, that sound helped me to concentrate on the message that was almost sticked in my mind.

"look for it," she said

At first, I didn't know what she was referring to, but after listening to her message for a while I realized what she meant.

"It's on the nightstand, be careful not to tear or poke a hole in it," she said too.

I was looking for the table, I went to her room and saw her, I immediately knew what she was trying to tell me, there was a laptop on the nightstand, the message was clear, it was the tool to find the meaning of the message.

"On the nightstand," she kept saying.

At that point I was looking online and I found an article by a researcher who was just giving a conference in the city, it caught my attention, but he did not have a pen to write down the address, I looked in the drawer of the table where usually It is usually there, there were many condoms, I took them out to check if suddenly there was something at the bottom and I found more condoms.

"On the nightstand," she kept saying

I put away the condoms, some were left out and the drawer was half closed, she was also an expert in making everything fit well and in its place, using the old concept of war, I pushed it with brute force and a pen fell from above the nightstand, coincidence or everything was pointing to find one of the most hidden secrets of all time, I got dressed and left without saying goodbye.

When I came out the streets were still dark, with a bit of
fog, but everything changed in a second as I stared at a girl
who was dressed sporty, she stared at me, she smiled at me.

"Hey can I ask you a question," she said

I looked at the time, I still had time to get to the conference,
so I said yes.

She approached me, sniffed my neck.

"Yeah," she said.

I was speechless, was it another kind of riddle?

She smiled

"Come on, I'll write you my number," she told me

I continued without moving, she took the book from my
hands, opened the pages, saw the numbers, shook her head
as if she had deciphered something.

At that point I cleared my throat.

"In a blank space," I said

She found it very funny, then she looked at me, kissed me on the cheek as she put the book back in my hands.

"You're on the right way," she said me before leaving smiling.

I looked at her whole body while I was walking, for a strange reason she had discovered the route very easily, that left me thinking for several blocks, I saw the book again, I opened it where she opened it, I saw the page that she took, the I smelled, now I understood what she was telling me, and yes! we were both on the right way.

From that point, the sun appeared magically, the streets were filled with people, cars and smoke; breathing the tranquility of the city, my steps automatically followed the route.

I was the first to arrive at the conference, there was a girl at the door taking a selfie, she had a lock of hair over her face, I was silent watching her, she pouted, I loved that.

"You're a model," I said her.

She was surprised at first, but then she smiled at me.

"Not, silly," she said me.

She had a very striking makeup in her eyes, which made me not stop staring at her.

She put her hand between her mouth and chin.

"so cute," I said her, because she actually looked like that, very cute

Without hesitation she had the ability to express herself in selfies.

She looked at me from head to toe.

"For the conference," she said me

I said yes with my whole body.

"It was postponed, you have to come in the afternoon," she said me while pretending to kiss.

I froze again.

She smiled to me.

"But I have something for you in compensation for getting up early "she said while handing me a book.

I received it with great affection, she noticed it, she smelled my neck, she kissed me gently.

"bye sweetie," she said as she walked in and closed the door.

It was another coincidence that I was only the only attendant at that time, and that she handed me the fabulous book, too much of a coincidence, I couldn't resist the temptation to read the book immediately, there was a very beautiful park with trees around that kindly extended a warm shade, I started reading like I had never done before, then I saw many things clearly, I was looking straight ahead for a moment and a guy with folders, posters, backpacks was in such a hurry that his wallet fell, I called him, but besides everything, he was wearing headphones, I had to jog for more than five blocks to give him the wallet, he took off one of the headphones, he was surprised, but then he was so happy that he gave me a business card from a company, it was a number and with the same digits, of course different order, this was another coincidence or I was on the right way.

What a good feeling I had in my chest, a good deed led to another, and now I had in my hands, one of the greatest clues that would allow me to continue on my path to the truth.

I went back wanting to jump, run and scream with happiness, but there were many people around and I regretted it for a moment, I said to myself, if they are thinking of millions of things at this precise moment, and if I jump on one foot, stick out the tongue at them, show them the middle finger, they will continue in their millions of thoughts, they would fake a smile, they would walk as if they had a date with someone important; I also kept saying inside of me, for example that girl who is sitting face down pretending to read, and at the same time paying attention to the guy who is recording her, by far, she'll see me and fill one of her thoughts with some part of me, maybe she's interested in my smile, my voice, or maybe just the card that is in my hands, while all that was passing through my mind, they were walking with gigantic steps, in less time than the girl spent lying down to stands up, laughing, and kissed the cameraman, the whole path was empty.

so, I jumped, I ran from side to side, and scream with happiness.

The girl in the example was watching me, she smiled at me, she was approaching me as if something was imminently attracting her, but the cameraman took her by the hand, made her run, jump, and scream.

They lasted less than three seconds in my thoughts, I managed to count ten; one when the girl was looking at me, another when the girl approached, kissed me and ran away, the third when she approached me looked at me with contempt, said crazy, and kissed me, from the fourth to the ten they were a little blurry sometimes I saw her lying in the meadow, sometimes on a beach, the last on a bed.

I was able to verify the veracity of my statements when my thoughts began to fill with numbers, the different combinations that I had deciphered, the card, the book I had in my hands, and the time I had to find the truth.

Without further pause I sat down again in the same place, because it was strategic, from there I saw the man who gave me such a clue, also because the shade that the tree gave was perfect for reading.

I read a few more pages, but I couldn't wait to call that number, for something fate put that good man on the park road, I held the card for more than a minute in my hand, because at that moment I pass a girl grimacing and looking away, I finally discarded her, when I realized that she was waiting for her two boyfriends.

I counted to ten before calling, a girl answered me, her

voice was pleasant, with all the calls I had made, I was already an expert in knowing personalities just by listening to her tone of voice, she allowed me to speak little, she told me that she was expecting me in half an hour, in an address that was precisely half an hour from there, one more coincidence or something predestined.

I walked without looking at anyone, just like when I was little and my mother told me not to talk to anyone, or to anything, in those young years I paid attention to not talking to anyone on the way, even with some classmates who were going on the same walk to school, they always thought that I was something hateful, and even strange, I look at them the same way, in my mind I told them, their mother didn't tell them not to talk to anyone, so listen to her , but I never said it out loud.

One thing in which I never obeyed my mother wasn't talking to anything, that part was great, it gave life to many objects that flew like in comic strips, the fact is that I didn't talk to anyone on the street, my mouth was sealed although I saw many beautiful girls pass by, one of them touched my buttocks, another half a kiss and hugged me, I was prepared with the weapons that the women always carry.

"I have a girlfriend and I love her. ya heard me!" I said to each one.

All of them stared at me for five seconds, then broke into a fit of laughter, one of the prettiest, had to ask another girl who passed for some water.

The girl stared at her, caught a slight level of laughter, then asked me.

"what happened to her?"

I was silent, I didn't want her to also have a similar attack, I looked into her eyes, touched her hand, as if to explain what had happened, suddenly she threw herself at me, she kissed me passionately, I kissed her for three minutes, then I used another weapon from them, I put my hands on her chest, I backed away.

"Wait, you're going so fast, and I like it slow, plus I'm engagement," I said.

I counted the seconds in which she stared at me without saying anything, I managed to reach six, when she exploded in a laugh, it was so impressive that the other girl who had already managed to control herself, couldn't stand it and again continued laughing until she fell into ground.

I looked at the time and I had only five minutes to go.

I wasn't going to get there on time, so I ran like I almost never do, I looked to one side and a girl in a sports suit that made her look very attractive, was running next to me, she smiled at me, but I avoided her and kept running

But she used a weapon that we use.

"Ugly," she yelled at me.

I immediately stopped, it made me really want to laugh, but I held back.

"You dropped this, ugly beautiful," she said as she handed me the card that I had dropped.

I didn't have no words to express her gratitude, she knew it, so she kissed me and slapped me.

"we're even" she said me and kept running.

I looked to the side and I had finally arrived, it was a huge theater, when I said the girl's name and showed the card, they led me to a very elegant office, they handed me a wireless microphone, a brochure, and they led me towards the theater by the doors behind the stage.

"it's your turn," they said me

They led me to the stage, it was full of audience, everyone clapping,

"but I do?" I said

"Talk about what you know, what you've learned" they said me

At first, I was nervous, but then remembering everything I had done, as I got to decipher the message, I also talked about the chapters of the book that I had read, I told jokes that I had never told, they applauded me for more than two minutes.

At the end of the event they led me through a dark corridor, the walls had phosphorescent numbers, I was looking at them carefully while the two girls that accompanied me changed their clothes.

Those numbers had the same digits, but some looked like letters, after several minutes my eyes saw the points run, the commas fly, until the girls held me very affectionately, we went out in the middle to a party where everyone was very elegant, I barely entered, five girls approached me.

"Can we take a picture with you?" They said.

"Why not?" I said to them.

One of them hugged me, kissed me on the mouth tenderly, but then the friends said something to her.

"Don't be silly," they said in chorus.

I looked at the two girls who came with me, they looked at me as if wanting to say, sign their autographs, but I didn't see where to sign their autograph, nor did I have a pen.

"Do it," the friends said to the girl.

I saw the girls again, my hostesses, they rolled their eyes and turned their backs on me.

There I understood everything, when I saw the whole place was full of very beautiful girls, they all looked at me as if they wanted to hear me say something, maybe act, or maybe?

Sure, that's what they told me.

I did a previous warm-up, some of them laughed when I moved my mouth gesturing, it is one of the most effective exercises for this type of event, a few of them broke into an attack of nervous laughter, they shook their heads as if they were dancing rock heavy, others as if they had seen some horror movie, but others were very serious, I just stayed watching them, to each one I spent two seconds intermittently, when I saw a girl again, she took off one garment.

I didn't observe them anymore when I felt a little dizzy.

At that moment, I looked at the girls, at my hostesses, they made me that gesture.

It was time to act, and I started to sign their autographs, I sweated like I had never done in my entire life, several of them wanted to take my pen, they found the way I wrote curious, they told me it was a particular way, that it had some magic.

In those moment, I laughed, but I was able to control myself I didn't want to look like the girls who had to pour a lot of water on themselves

After signing too many autographs, which I don't really know how I did it, to get in good with all of them, but it turned out perfect, the numbers had also helped me to perfect my calligraphy, my style and my punctuation.

Then my hostesses led me down another corridor, it was very bright and elegant, they sat with me in a very spacious room, I began to read the book while they processed my first payment for having fun on stage, I discovered other interesting titles.

The three days I had to solve everything have turned into months, I have read more than a hundred books, from each one I extracted a small part that I have applied to the riddle, and I'm only one number away from finding out the whole truth.

and I know where exactly It's, she has the answer, I'm finally ready to face her again.

There she was, as if she knew everything, she was in the same place, at the appointed time, with the pose she should be doing, many nights I dreamed how she looks at me at this moment.

She's leaning against the wall number ninety-nine, looking at me with an eight hundred and eighty-eight, her white blouse discloses the contour of her wonderful breasts, her sexy glasses point to zero-zero.

And her lips?

Her lips are the color of five, her sensual black miniskirt is the sign of three, the same digit that would take me months to decipher.

I'm finally face to face with the truth, I can finally see with the clarity of the sparkle in her eyes.

She stares at me as I approach, I don't know if she noticed that now I'm different, that I have also changed the way I walk, speak, perceive things.

Yes!

She gave me the signal, I know, the nod of approval to enter her life, and thus together untangle our puzzles helping humanity.

Yes!

She already knows, that's why she gave me the numbers, that's why she did it, that's why she chose me among her millions of followers, that privilege I earned with honors, also with the satisfaction of many laughs, bright eyes, and signed autographs.

"Hi," I say as I hold one of her hands.

She blushed, I think she was shocked that I had solved the riddle, because she was silent.

"It took me longer than I thought, but I figured it out," I said to her.

She pretended not to know what I was talking about, I like that the mystery is preserved, it's part of the last riddle, I know, I have become very insightful in those details, so I gave her the sheet that she gave me that day with a happy face added in the end.

There she realized everything, she looked into my eyes as if reading my memories, she went by the hours I spent staying up late, for the YouTubers, for the stories they told, for the melodramas that helped me find courage, she also laughed as if would have been in class or in one of the auditoriums.

Her beautiful laugh continued for a few more seconds, I waited for everything to calm down, I didn't want her to give her a mad laugh attack and then I said.

"the digit three was the hardest,"

She looked at me as if I was crazy, that enchanted me because it is a sign that I'm her only one.

"Did you call this number?" she told me

That question was certainly in some other sense.

"Yes," I said to her.

she smiled and turned away.

"Hey, sorry, I gave you a fake number, I gotta go," she said to me.

Her cheeks reddened and her hands shook a little.

so, I knew.

I held one of her hands with some force and made her take a step towards me, then I kissed her, then she looked into my eyes, and there she knew that I had deciphered it, there she knew that I was the only one who could do it, then she kissed me with the passion of a true love.

Stories full of secrets, of enigmas, of the mystery that is hidden in the lyrics
of the poems.
Sensually woven around emotions, feelings, dreams, and desires.

Thank You !

I hope you enjoyed :)

www.JohnM3Frame.com